With warm hugs and lots of wishes

to _____

from _____

Rock-a-bye, Lambie-pie

illustrated by
michel bernstein

Andrews and McMeel
A Universal Press Syndicate Company
Kansas City

ISBN: 0-8362-4727-2

Rock-a-bye,
Lambie-pie

Strawberry, blueberry,
mulberry stew—
Who rules the kingdom
of Kalamazoo?

Who goes to London
to chat with the Queen,
Sails to China
and ports in between...

Swings on a star
in a summertime sky...

Visits the Man in the Moon
way up high?

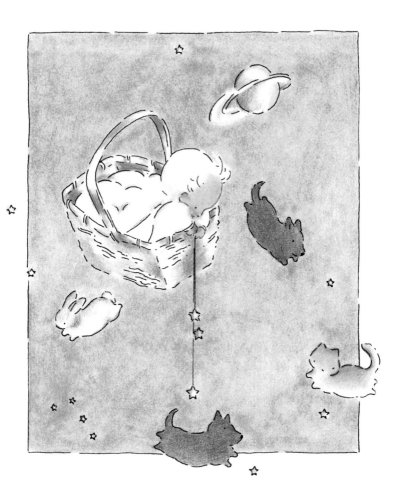

La-dee-da, tweedledee,
hullabaloo—
What baby's learning
to play peekaboo?

*Who chases butterfly
fairies with glee,
Bounces to Boston
upon mommie's knee...*

Learns about what-nots,
etceteras, and such,
Calms the wild beast
with one baby-soft touch?

Button nose, baby clothes,
little white shoes —
You can have all the
adventures you choose.

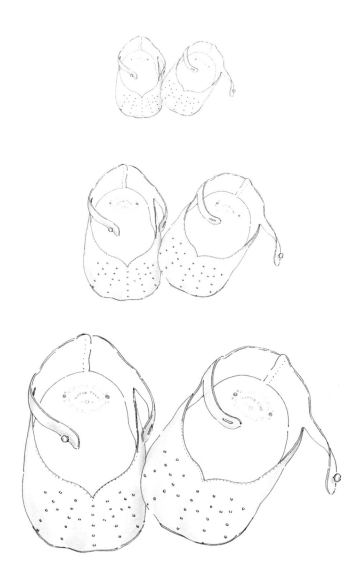

*Fly on a gander
through dreamland at night,
Play with the sandman
until morning light...*

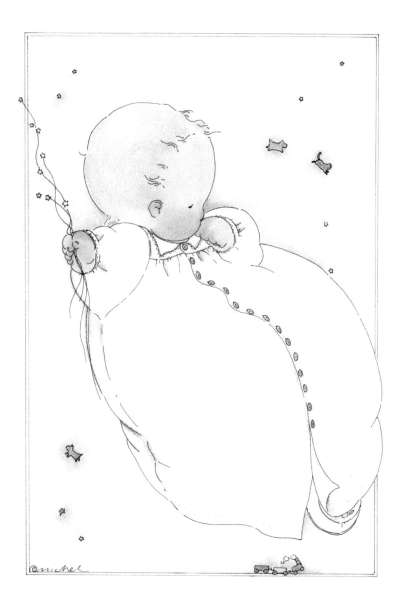

Cuddle a dilly-down-ducky
at dawn,
Ride a fine carriage
out onto the lawn.

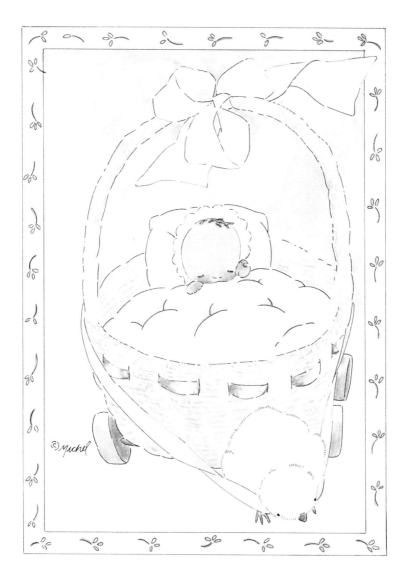

Rock-a-bye, lambie-pie,
all pink and blue—
Wonderful worlds lie
waiting for you!

Soar with the words
of each story and poem,
Far from your nursery,
miles from your home...

Carried on wings
of each fanciful rhyme,
Till the tale ends...

...and it's
beddy-bye time.

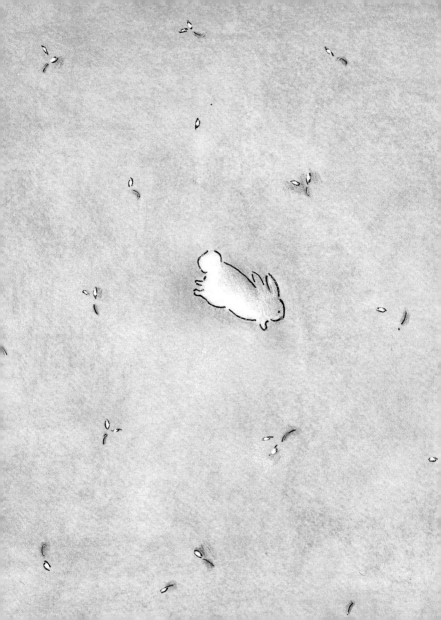